# The
# Midwife's
# Tale
# and
# Other
# Christmas
# Stories

Stonework Press
5705 Crestview Avenue
Indianapolis, IN  46220

© 1993 by W. Edward Harris

ISBN 0-9638864-2-8

# • TABLE OF CONTENTS •

*****

## DEDICATION

*****

*****

# Dedication

For my grandmother Della Harris of Daylight, Tennessee, mother of nine, midwife to hundreds in Warren County.

# A FEW WORDS OF INTRODUCTION

Who really knows about the birth of Jesus? The four Gospel writers - Matthew, Mark, Luke and John - have different versions of the events surrounding the birth of Jesus of Nazareth. Besides these four versions we have created a modern version that emphasizes certain elements of the Gospel stories and ignores others. James Efird of Duke University Divinity School calls this version a *"Fifth Gospel."* It is a pretty version that lacks the gritty truth. It doesn't have the smell of the stables, a crying baby, unruly crowds, cruel soldiers and all the harsh anxiety of giving birth in primitive conditions.

The birth place of Jesus was not likely to have been a stable or barn but rather a hillside cave where animals were sheltered. The shepherds were probably not a devout group but rather an unsavory bunch.

Each of the four Gospels focuses on a different part of the story. Matthew highlights Joseph's uncertainties, the visit of the Magi, the flight into Egypt and the slaughter of the innocents. The latter story is too shocking to modern sensibilities to get much attention in spite of the fact that we live in the century of Holocausts, Gulags, atomic war and mass murder of every kind.  Mark skips the birth story altogether and starts with the baptism of Jesus.  His emphasis is on the mission and ministry.  Luke reflects on Mary's experience.  John analyzes the theological meanings.

All close readers and students of the Bible have long been troubled by the conflicting accounts of ancestry of Jesus.  Matthew and Luke give differing accounts of his Davidic ancestry tracing it through both Joseph and Mary.

Most scholars today are satisfied that the birth stories were not part of the earliest Christian tradition.  The Resurrection was the key issue of the early church as well as the general expectation of the return of the Messiah.

The question of Jesus' birth and origins is probably a "*second generation*" concern arising 30 to 50 years after his death.  It probably arose as a way to explain how the Messiah was both human and divine.  The writer of Luke gives us a clue to his method when he says he has "*investigated carefully*" in order to write "*the exact truth*" about events he had not personally witnessed.  It is here that my stories take off.  I have tried to imagine how members of the early church who were known as Followers of The Way might have gone about trying to determine the events of Jesus' birth. In most of the stories there is an anonymous and unseen person writing down the story. You will hear echoes of the Gospel accounts as you see the birth story through the eyes of Mary's little brother, the inn keeper's son, a Roman soldier, a crippled shepherd boy, and the midwife who delivered the baby among the animals of the stable.

These stories are the way it might have been. As such they contain my own emphases of the philosophical and theological meaning of the birth story. I've told these stories in church usually on the Sunday before Easter or on Christmas Eve. Ministers of various faiths have used them with good success. They seem to travel well. Several years ago an edition of three hundred stories similar to this was issued. Since then I have written new versions and added additional details. I tend to rewrite them each time I tell the story. I hope they are improved. I have attempted to expunge all anachronisms. In an earlier version I characterized Mary's mother as a "*romantic*" and the sparks from the sheep's fur as "*electricity*." I hope you will not find any of these gaffes although I've left one in for people who like to find such errors. I am one of these persons, too.

The stories are essentially the remembrances of older people recalling a particular moment in their long lives which holds greater interest for other people than for themselves.

* * * * * * * * * *

There is a sixth story, a little "*lagniappe*", which is a New Orleans word meaning "*a little extra thrown in.*" It is typically a deal sweetener. This is a more modern story although it is getting pretty old itself. It's about "*The First Christmas After the War*" and a ten-year-old boy experiencing Christmas in all its magic. The story has its own tragic undertones of the quiet abuse of the innocents. I add it because it is what Christmas means to me - service to the poor and needy, family closeness, presents, surprises and the ambiguities of human existence. It sounds like too much for such a simple story to bear, but this one is true, as true as one's own experience and memory can make it.

W. Edward Harris

# IT'S A MIRACLE

Joseph, who was the father of Yeshua and husband of my sister Mary was a very strange person indeed. When I was yet a young boy, Joseph was very old. I believe that when I was 12 he must have been 50 years of age. We young boys thought of the carpenter as a crazy man. Certainly he was dreamy and absent-minded, and paid no attention at all to his business. He came to Nazareth from the town of Bethlehem and set up as a carpenter, making chairs, tables, and farm implements. He was a very good carpenter but very independent. He had no permanent workplace at first, but later had a small shop in the lower part of his house. Once my father sent me to get him to come to the fields to repair a broken ox yoke. I was told to ask him to hurry to where my father was working. He told me, "*I shall come day after tomorrow.*"

"*But,*" I protested, "*my father says to come now.*"

"*I shall come day after tomorrow.*"

He was a strange one and my father harbored some bitterness toward him for this refusal.

Joseph was not the only carpenter in the town but he did little to win business. He would often go out into the hills around the town and wander aimlessly. Some said he talked with birds and animals and he was well-known for his knowledge of the ways of creatures.

Another time he was asked to estimate and make a bid on some repairs to the town hall where the council met. My father was the chairman of the committee. Joseph appeared before them, but told them, "*I do not bid. If you want me to do the work I shall. If not, get someone else.*"

"*Independent,*" my father called him. "*Dreamy and stupid,*" my mother called him. He was not well-liked and did not mingle with the men as they gathered for drinks at the local inn. He was aloof and had no one as a friend at all. He wasn't married and never had been. Occasionally one or the other of the widows of the town would have him to supper but nothing ever came of it. None of this would be of any importance except for what happened later.

My mother always thought of him as an outsider, since he was not born in Nazareth. My mother never trusted anyone who was not born in our town. Why I'll never know, because Nazareth was a den of thieves and robbers. Some of the fathers of a den of thieves and robbers. Some of the fathers of my friends were farmers who also were robbers along the highway. Others received and re-sold merchandise from those who stole. I never heard my mother mutter a word against any of them. I know now that we had a hard life when I was a boy. The Romans were harsh in their rule, despising us, and taking all they could of the harvest and sales of goods for taxes. My father was a prosperous farmer through the good fortune of having all his brothers die before they came of age; thus he inherited a sizable farm. Neither I nor my sister Mary ever lacked for anything. We lived in a large and comfortable house of nine rooms and were considered wealthy enough to be required to quarter soldiers in our home.

My sister Mary was three years older than I and if anyone had ever said she would wind up marrying old Joseph the carpenter, they would have been thought daft. My mother would have been wild with indignation. My sister was known for her beauty and great skills at cooking, sewing, and keeping house. My mother was always carrying on about how gentle, how beautiful and wonderful Mary was. Mary always did a great deal of work at home and in the fields. We all worked in those days, even children. It is not like it is now.

You never know when you become aware of some things, but for as long as I can remember my mother would talk about the man Mary would marry. My mother had a list of acceptable possible husbands. All of them were the sons of merchants who were better off than we. I knew all of them even though they were older than I was. There was Gabriel and Joshua, brothers, the sons of Minikah, the wealthiest farmer of the town, and the Roman's mayor. There was the silversmith's son, Hiram, and the Rabbi's son, Telusha. The Rabbi's son was the youngest, 17, and I hated him for he was a bully and a braggart. I don't care if he was a Rabbi's son. These were the men my mother said were fine young men and acceptable husbands for her daughter. Mary was 15 and in those days we married quite young, if we got married. I used to tease my mother to tell me who she thought I should marry, who she had on my list, but she'd never say. Luckily I got out of Nazareth before she could get a wife for me.

I was always teasing Mary about those "*acceptable*" husbands. Hiram was called "*Ears*" by us boys because he had the largest pair of ears I've ever seen on a human being. I guess little brothers have been doing this for years. Gabriel and Joshua had great rounded heads typical of all in their family. Telusha had a nose that dominated his face.

I would say something like:

*"Mary, I saw Ears today."*

She'd be interested but pretend not to be.

*"Oh, what was he doing?"*

*"Running errands for his father. He was flying around town, his ears flapping in the breeze so that his feet were fairly off the ground."*

*"Don't be stupid, Aaron,"* she'd say to me.

*"Some kind of children you'll get from a flopped-eared one like Hiram."*

Then she'd blush and call to mother and tell her I was thinking impure thoughts. My mother very much disliked impure thoughts and she would have my father whip me.

My father later attributed the whole mess to my mother and I suppose he was right. My mother was a dreamer and quite unrealistic. She believed in love. Rather than have my father meet with the family of the husband-to-be and work out the dowry and financial arrangement, as was the custom and practice, my mother wanted Mary to choose the man she'd marry. Mary knew all of them, having grown up with them and seen them in temple school and she knew their sisters quite well. My mother's plan was to invite each of the "*acceptable*" men to have dinner at the house. At the end of the four week period, Mary would choose. My father protested, but one by one they came.

My mother was anxious to get the matter settled for we had living with us a Roman soldier, Quintus Marcellus, who was a strikingly handsome soldier, very strong, possessing a sweet nature and very kind. Mary, I know, liked him. My mother later said she was "*afraid something would happen.*" We knew to keep our distance with the Roman soldiers because they were unpredictable and could be ruthless. Marcellus was not really a Roman but from a country far to the North of Rome called Helvetia. He was fair-skinned with striking blue eyes. Among us boys we hated the Romans and used to dream of the day when we'd grow up and drive the Romans out of our land. But some of the Romans were all right and Marcellus was one of them.

No one really knows what happened but it happened. After the four had been to the house -- Hiram, Gabriel, Joshua and Telusha -- Mary was to make up her mind. Mary though could not choose or would not. She first named Gabriel; then Hiram;

then Telusha. My father was impatient with the whole process and told Mary, *"You're not getting any younger my fine smart lady. The way your mother has spoilt you, I don't know that any of them will have you."* My father held for the old ways in all things.

One day soon after this my father saw Mary coming from the fields walking hand in hand with Gabriel. He came home and announced to Mother that it was settled. He was going that day to call on Gabriel's father, Minikah, and make the arrangements. It seemed settled until Mary came home. There was a great scene with my father raving and shouting, Mary and mother crying, and in the end my father shouting, *"damnable nonsense, damnable nonsense! Of course no young girl can make up her mind. That is why the parents should make the decisions!"*

He went out of the house and down to the inn where the men gathered to drink in the habit of men from time immemorial.

A month went by and then another, and still there was no decision. My father harvested his wheat and made a good deal in the sale and came home with several silver coins. He was in a bright and happy mood and suggested that in order to get

Mary to make a decision they should have the round of "*acceptables*" to supper again.

"*That might not be a bad idea,*" my mother said.

There was something in my mother's voice that caused my father to ask, "*What's wrong?*"

"*The child's with child,*" my mother said.

For a full minute my father said nothing and then mockingly repeated "*The child's with child. You mean that our daughter, this young woman is pregnant.*"

Turning to Mary he demanded: "*Who is it?*"

Mary sat at the table eating a piece of bread. "*Who's what?*" she said sulkily.

"*Who's the father?*"

"*I don't know.*"

"*It is Gabriel,*" my father said, seizing on the one observable sign he had. "*Oh, my God, Marcellus? No, it can't be. Who? Who is it?*"

*"I don't know, father."*

*"Who have you lain with, child?"*

*"No one,"* said Mary.

*"Have you lain with them all?"*

*"No,"* she said.

*"Who, child, who? Name one. This decides it."*

*"I don't know. I have known none of them,"* said Mary.

*"What in God's name do you mean, child?"* father said.

*"Mary, Mary,"* my mother moaned.

I stood by confused by the whole proceeding, but knowing that something most terrible had happened.

*"Don't bother her now,"* my mother said. *"She is tired. She is telling the truth."* My mother half believed her story.

Father said: "*Now is the time for you to tell us, Mary, I am not going to stand for this. Your mother has brought this about with her fine plans. I am going to Minikah tonight and name Gabriel as the father. We can smooth it over, you are not the first bride to carry a child. It happens, it happens, it happens,*" he said, repeating the phrase for the comfort it seemed to give him.

That night he went to the home of Minikah and told him of his suspicions. Gabriel was called in and denied having touched Mary. My father recounted the hand-holding incident but Gabriel told of the gossip about Mary's being with other men in the town. So Father made the round of the families getting denials and hearing yet more gossip and tales of Mary.

He threatened Mary. He wanted to send her away to his sister but still Mary would name no one. My father cross-questioned Marcellus but it was clear that he stood innocent.

I never felt closer to my sister than I did at this time. She seemed so helpless and in so much trouble. My mother seemed helpless too. Everywhere in the town there was talk of Mary. She'd always been spoken of, but now she was the butt of jokes: Would the baby have ears like Hiram, blue eyes like Marcellus, the distinctive nose of Telusha, and so on.

My mother ignored it all, fluttering and hovering around her daughter. My father carried himself in such a way that all talk ceased wherever he went. My father was deeply hurt.

Mary simply brooded and then she fell ill. Finally the story emerged which I first heard from my friend Abraham, who heard it from his sister. This was the story of the angel or spirit who had come to Mary to tell her she would be mother to a great leader who would be the Messiah.

"*The Messiah,*" I gasped, when Abraham told me. I wondered with Abraham if the angel could be the father. Later I heard the same story and many variations. Mary herself told me the story about her vision and it wasn't like any of the stories but it was similar. Soon the story was all around the town and it was cause of still more joking, although some took it seriously.

My mother believed the story. She told it to my father who said, "*Has it come to this? Has it come to this?*" It was my mother, I believe, who made up the story in the first place and persuaded Mary that it happened in that way. During this time

Mary did very little. She sat quietly all day and wept and then she'd sleep only to wake and weep still more. The visits of her girlfriends helped to cheer her and in a few weeks she was feeling a good deal better.

Mary held to her story and some of her friends believed it too. Our cousin Elizabeth, who was married and pregnant, said that she had seen an angel too. She had a very involved story. My mother dismissed it and Elizabeth by saying she was "*jealous*" of Mary, although why this might be was never clear. My father said Elizabeth was trying to be kind.

My father took charge and announced that Mary must be married. He said he would find her a husband. Mary did not resist but Mother insisted on giving her approval. Father dismissed her as having done enough.

"*Who do you have in mind?*" my mother asked.

"*Joseph, the carpenter,*" father said.

"*No! Oh, no!*" exclaimed mother.

"*But you overlook the fact that our lovely Mary is not quite so desirable as a wife. That could be any man's baby she carries. God knows who the demented woman has slept with. And the angel story. I shall handle this in my own way."*

*"But Joseph is an old man,"* my mother said.

*"He shall be good enough, but even Joseph shall have to be persuaded. For this I will need your help, your cooperation. Let us make a little plan to catch this dreamy carpenter."*

My mother's love of plans, intrigues and plots overcame her aversion to outsiders for she recognized that Mary would have to be married.

It was really quite easy as it worked out. Joseph was invited to the house. My mother flattered and made over the carpenter. Mary sat subdued and quiet. Following supper the carpenter and my father sat before the fire. My father outlined the situation and made him a straight proposition on the dowry and marriage settlement. My father knew his man for Joseph's reply was immediate and perfect, reassuring my mother and pleasing my father: *"I will love the girl and care for her. The child will be as my own."* That was all he said. It was settled.

The wedding date was set and the marriage of Mary and Joseph accomplished. Mary was neither sad nor happy but accepted the whole thing without protest.

That was the way it was. It seems strange that it is so but it is. My nephew who was called Yeshua was born in the town of Bethlehem where Joseph had gone for the tax enrollment called by the Romans. This fact should have ruined the baby in the eyes of my mother but she loved the child more than she ever loved me, her own son. When they came home the whole town searched for signs of the true paternity of the baby. There were no physical characteristics to suggest any one in particular but some people found signs for all of the men in turn.

The story of the birth of Yeshua I know nothing of directly. When they returned from Bethlehem, Mary told the now well-known story of wise men, kings following a star and shepherds visiting the baby. Mary delivered the child in a stable, which always worried my mother. The stories of kings coming and angels singing at the birth of Yeshua were strange enough, but not so strange as the jewels and precious spices and ointments Joseph and Mary brought home. Mary said they were gifts of the kings. Even Joseph said so.

My mother said, "*It is a miracle, a miracle, a promise from God fulfilled; he will be a great leader of the people.*"

My father said, "*Yes, considering all that happened, it is a miracle.*"

My father lived to be 95 and always loved Yeshua in spite of all the trouble he got into later.

# THAT'S THE WAY IT HAPPENED

My grandchildren will be coming soon and they will ask me again to tell them the story about the time I was a boy in Bethlehem. They never tire of the story of the time when I saw the great kings come to the inn my father owned, how the star shone in the sky, and how I saw a child born in the stable behind the inn. And their eyes light up at the story of the gold -- no more so than my eyes lit up -- probably because it was a sight to see. But I get ahead of myself.

They will be coming and they will want to hear the story again. To them and to many other people now this is the most important thing about me -- that I was there in the stable the night the one they call Jesus -- and the Messiah -- was born. I was there and they like to hear the story but they don't pay any attention to me. It does not matter that I have lived now to be 76 years old and that I have seen many, many strange things in my life. Things more strange than the star. Yes they'll listen to the stories about the birth and the star and the kings coming but they don't pay any attention to the fact that those were hard times. In those days people worked. Not like today. People just slide by, never paying any attention. In those days, you didn't work, you didn't eat. From the time I was eight years old I was doing the work of a man. You had to. There was no other way. My father was a good man. He was not even a hard or vicious man but he put me to working and doing the work of a man when I was eight. No, they don't want to hear about the work. Nor do they want to hear about the people who starved in those days ... the lepers and the cripples that were everywhere, and the crazy mad men who roamed the streets and would just as soon kill you as look at you. And you couldn't travel. You didn't dare travel because of the thieves and robbers that lurked along every major road in Judea and all of Palestine. And the cruel Herods -- father and son -- they don't want to hear that. All they can remember now is that they were Jews and rebuilt the Temple at Jerusalem. They get the credit but it was from taxes pulled out of the people. They think we have high taxes today. In those days, believe me, it was worse. They took the taxes and then you might eat. And your taxes did nothing but be used to pay the expenses of the Roman's ruler, to finance the army which helped extract those taxes, and to pay the tax collectors and to be sent off as tribute to Rome. No, people don't want to hear about those days. And the fights. Everybody was in a group and organized to fight every other group and we could never get together against the Romans -- they played us all off against one another. There was a time when we rose up but I don't want to talk about that.

Well, I'm babbling on. My wife Martha says I talk too much. And that I should watch my tongue. I'm doing that. But, I ask you what are they going to do to an old man? Kill me. Ha! No, when I was a boy times were very different. I pity my grandchildren and even my children if we should ever go back to the way things were. They could not survive. They have had everything too easy. Too much and too easy. I guess it is my fault too. But what are you supposed to do for your family? Still, they are so soft and so innocent. They know nothing of the hardness of the world, the meanness of people.

I have grandchildren now and daughters-in-law who are caught up in this Messiah thing. They think the Messiah has come. They pride themselves on knowing me because they know I was there when their Messiah was born. I've never gone in for Temple. I guess you'd say I was not a good Jew. But I've always paid my part and supported the Temple. And I say my prayers but this more out of respect for my parents than anything else. For a chosen people we have sure been put through a lot of persecution and torture. The Romans ran our Temples as long as they were here. They controlled everything. Now I've got grandchildren who are Christians and it's spreading. It's madness. Of course I told the boys to stay away from these girls; Nazarene girls. They come from good families. Nice girls, but, you know, not quite right. And their parents too, not quite right. Nazarenes. I don't know about some people. Everybody's a little strange. But now we've got Christian grandchildren -- me and Martha -- and are they Jews? Have they been circumcised? I'm afraid to ask. That's the way it is. You get afraid to ask. Such craziness there is, you don't want to hear it.

My boys though, they are all right. They work hard, they take care of their families and that's good. And who, I ask you, can control a wife? I have been married nearly sixty years and you think I have nothing to say on that topic?

But this Christian thing is catching on. Not only here but all over the Empire. I traveled a lot when I was younger and you'd find them meeting everywhere -- Jerusalem -- a big group at one time -- Antioch, Alexandria, Athens, and even into Rome. Still, I don't think it's the same as being a Jew.

One thing I do know and that is how it all got started. I remember now even though it was years ago. One of the fisherman from Judea, John Mark, wanted to get my story. I read what he wrote. It's pretty close, but then he wasn't there and he didn't get it quite right. Anyway, the Christians know I was present at the birth of their Messiah so they are always coming around and asking me about it. I've told the story a lot and I have to admit I've changed it a little bit from time to time. You get tired of telling the same story all the time. But if you get a Christian coming into town they will likely look me up and try to get me to tell the story. Sometimes I tell them and sometimes I don't. I always demand to know if they are Jews. The Messiah has to be a Jew, doesn't he? We're the chosen ones in trouble.

I guess I ought to tell the story. I should try to put it down right, once and for all. My daughter-in-law Ann wants me to write it down. I keep figures good but I don't write so well. In my line of work, trading oil and wine, you need to count, but you don't need to write so good.

I'm dictating this to the person -- what's your name? -- Samuel -- that she sent over to get this whole story down. He's doing a good job. You are getting all of this down aren't you? Write it all down, especially the part about the taxes. And the work.

It was in the spring of 3741 during the reign of Caesar Augustus that the taxes became worse. I can remember my father complaining. Then it was decided that everybody would have to go to the home city in which they were born and be re-enrolled on the tax rolls. Everybody. It was to be a census and tax enrollment. My father ran an inn. We lived upstairs in a group of rooms and we rented out nearly forty rooms. I was working cleaning and sweeping in the inn from the time I was able to carry a broom. Before I ever went to any kind of school I was working. The week of the census I have never seen so many people. Bethlehem is one of those places it was good to be from and everybody left if they could. So they had to come back for the census. Right away my father realized we would have to make room for the travelers. My brothers and I gave up our rooms and they were rented out. Every room had more than one or two persons in them. Straw pallets were laid end to end in the rooms and in the halls. We packed the people in. In some of the stories I've seen, they've tried to make my father to be a bad man because he turned away the couple from Nazareth, Mary and Joseph. They arrived late and there wasn't any place for them. It was Mother who suggested that they be put in the stable and that's where I was sleeping since I'd rather have been there than with my brother Shmuel. I was told to move a Roman's soldier's horse out of the one of the stalls, which I did. The stable was pretty nice. My father told me to look after them and to let him know when the baby was to come. That really excited me. That was a very big thing for me. I'd seen all kinds of animals born, but I'd never seen a human baby born. Although even I could tell it wouldn't be long. The woman was tired from riding on a donkey which they called Zeno. I was the one that led them back to the stable and helped them get unloaded and all set up. I was the one who carried the water for the animals and I was the one that got food for them after the cooks had gone home. The man Joseph was a carpenter from Nazareth and a nice man too. He was a strong man. You could see huge muscles in his arms and he had little jokes he would tell. And riddles. A lot of people forget old Joseph, but I'll tell you one thing, the baby looked exactly like him. And that's important since a lot of people have tried to make up other stories. But I was there and I know what I saw.

When the baby was coming it was Joseph who sent me for the midwife and the midwife who set me to bringing water from the kitchen. I was there in time to see the baby born. You can see it a hundred times and there's just nothing like it. Red and scrawny at the first, the baby cleaned up real nice and was beautiful, seeming to have a shiny glow about him. The birth of a baby brings out all kinds of people and because there were so many people in Bethlehem it was like a carnival. My father came and tried to drive the people away. He asked Joseph if there was anything they needed and if there was anything he could do for them and Joseph said "*no.*" My father left me in charge, in case anything should come up.

And things did come up. We had quite a crowd of visitors there that night. I'll never forget it. First came a big bunch of my people I knew, friends of my brothers and shepherds from the surrounding countryside who'd come to be taxed. They might have been drinking. But they were singing and telling all kinds of stories about what they'd heard in the wind while tending their flocks. They'd heard angels singing that told them to go to see the little new-born boy in our stable.

About the same time out in the front of the inn there arrived some kings from some far off small countries. Kings, I don't consider all of those people from little countries kings but they were nice enough . . . one was black as coal . . . and they had to see the baby. I'll never forget them coming in and bringing all sorts of presents to the mother, baby and the father. It's hard now to estimate what it was worth but some of the boxes were covered with gold and quite valuable. The story about there being a new baby born in the stable was spread around town. Joseph took all of these visitors pretty well, but he began to ask people to leave and I tried to assert myself as the one in charge and told them to go. "*It's the Messiah . . . the promised one,*" one of the shepherds told me, as he was leaving. And the kings, or potentates, or whatever they were, said they had come from the East, following the light of the star for days. They were sure it was some important astrological event.

We finally got them all out and I went up in the loft and lay there watching the mother nurse the baby. Joseph asked me a riddle: "*What is the toughest and gentlest thing in the world?*" I told him I didn't know. "*Think on it,*" he said. "*I'll tell you the answer in the morning.*"

As I lay there thinking, I remembered that I was in trouble because I'd moved the Roman soldier's horse. I fell asleep knowing that tomorrow I'd have to face a scolding.

I woke up the next morning hoping that maybe Joseph and his family would leave before the soldier got up. That was not possible and as the Roman soldier came and discovered his horse had spent the night outside he was furious. He demanded to know who had moved his horse. He threatened Joseph but the carpenter stood up to him and the Roman knew he was picking on the wrong man. He quickly surmised that it was me who moved the horse and he began to hit me. When I began my explanations, and I was a smooth talker even in those days, it only made him madder and he hit me and screamed "*I'll cut out your lying Jewish tongue.*" He then hit me again. He ran back toward the inn. I stood with Joseph and wondered what I was to do. Joseph told me not to be afraid. The soldier, Quintus was his name, came running back to the stable with a knife in his hand. Behind him were other Roman soldiers. I ran but too late -- they all three caught up to me and Quintus put his hand into my mouth and pulled my tongue out and prepared to cut it. My father had arrived by then and Joseph too. One or the other of them reached out and took the Roman soldier's arm and held back the knife. I slipped away. My father took responsibility for the horse incident and gave the soldier and his companions their lodgings free of charge.

My wife Martha thinks to this day that this is why I talk too much. And tell stories that run on and on. It's possible.

But that is the way Jesus, who is called the Messiah, was born. And I was there. You can see that I remember more about the soldier's trying to cut my tongue out than I might about some of the other things.

The Romans haven't been all bad. In some ways they have been good for business. The years I traveled selling wine and oil and a few tents and rugs were largely made possible by the Roman peace. But it was a harsh peace. I once walked the road from Sepphoris to Nazareth when it was lined with the crucified bodies of 1,000 Jews who had tried to rebel against the Romans. Yes, they could be hard. I hope my grandchildren don't have to see anything like that kind of slaughter.

My grandchildren always want to know if the soldier really might have cut my tongue off. Now, today, I don't know. But, then I was sure of it.

They don't know the evil and harshness of this world. And maybe that's all right.

What? Yes, the toughest and gentlest thing in the world? Yes, Joseph told me. *"It's love."* The Christians I tell this story to always take great stock by that. One told me I could have been the first Christian martyr if the Roman had cut my tongue out. That's not likely since I still stick with the law of Moses.

That's the way it happened and that's the way I remember it. If it helps anybody to know this I'm glad. Now that my grandchildren can read this maybe their mothers won't let them come to see me, so they don't have to hear the other stories I tell.

# THEY CALL ME QUINTUS

They call me Quintus Marcellus. My father named me. My troops called me Quintus. I have been in the service of Caesar for now nearly forty years, since I was 18. I am 58 and glad to be alive when most of the friends of my youth are dead. I am as happy and contented as I have ever been in my life. This is due to my lovely wife Julia. Because of the extraordinary life I have led and because there are people who seem interested, I have been asked to put down my story. Usually people are divided into two groups: the good and the bad or those who prefer one thing or its opposite. I have always divided people into three groups: those who make things happen; and those who watch things happen; and the overwhelming majority who have no idea what is happening. I've always been one who makes things happen.

It is strange how you can live your whole life and all of it is important to you, but one incident, one moment in time, even after forty years, still holds the center of the stage of your mind. I have soldiered in all parts of the Empire; I have been wounded many times and I hold the highest decorations and responsibilities that a non-Roman can hold in the Army. I am a native of Helvetia, but like my father before me, I have served in the armies of Rome. I consider myself a Roman. I have fought on the frontiers in Spain and all the way to India, but now as I recall my adventures and my life, I remember the time when I was beginning. I was sent out from Rome to Judea -- land of the Jews. I was young and ambitious. My father had convinced me this was the life and the way to advance was diligence in performance of one's duty. It was so many years ago. I shudder now to think of how young and how wild of spirit I was. Coming across on the ship, the old Judean hands, of which I am one now, regaled us with stories of the insane, crazy behavior of the Jews. They told us of the fights, the uprisings, that were inevitable among the people we would have a part in governing. Augustus was Emperor and Herod the First was King of Judea. My first station was in a little town away from Jerusalem in what has got to be one of the most desolate spots on the earth. My initial impression of the place of the town and the surrounding countryside was one of emptiness and utter waste. As I got to know it better, the people were quite lively, but in a way that can only be described as crazy. My first day on duty I saw men on the streets calling out the sins and faults of every person who would pass. They would run after them, pointing their fingers, shouting at them *"Repent, liar!" "Repent, harlot!"* They would hit one another. They would spit on one another. They would argue with one another in the streets. Most of these arguments centered around their peculiarly Jewish ideas of God. Forty years later this is what I remember: the shouting, the fighting, the vicious condemnations, the curses they flung at one another. There is nothing a soldier hates more than to become involved in settling these petty arguments. For who is to say who is right and who is wrong? It is worse than family fights when at least you know to protect the woman and let the man save face. Oh, the town? Nazareth.

The local populace and indeed the whole population hated us Romans, but I believe they would have torn one another apart if we hadn't been there. They hated you so much you soon came to despise them even if you started out thinking differently. From my youth up my father had encouraged me in the ideas of the famous Platonic teachers of the Stoa, who taught the ideas of universal brotherhood and the equality of all people. But we Romans were only the last of a long line of foreign invaders and rulers in Judea -- first Assyria, then Babylonia, then Persia, Alexander, and now Rome. Absorbed in local fights and feuds, the Jews were easily conquered. I now know much about those arguments about God, angels, the evil one, the Messiah who was coming, the fate of the soul after death, but for me then it all seemed crazy. The Pharisees, who seemed to be the dominant group, took great delight in being good, in claiming for themselves a kind of priority in the holy economy of God which was about to be brought to pass, and when we, the Romans, would be driven out of the land and into the sea. The Sadducees, yet another group, hated the Pharisees for their stupidity on a number of points, which should not detain us here since they lie so far in the past. It was to me, a new soldier and a young man on his first assignment, utter madness. But a soldier's routine doesn't change and soon we were used to all of the bizarre goings on. The truth is there was a lot of other activity and life in these communities and soon we settled down to garrison life with its rounds of patrols, exercise, practice in weapons and hard drinking. The liquor of Galilee is without exception the worst in the world. What we talked about was home, fighting, and our commander. These are things soldiers have talked about since the beginnings of time. And, yes, of course we talked about women and, in the manner of the young, did more talking than acting. It was not a good practice to become involved with the local girls. There were and are good reasons for prohibiting and preventing any kind of relationships between soldiers and local girls, but, as in all times, these sound policies have been violated in practice, but I suspect, to lesser extent than all the barracks talk would have you believe. At Nazareth we were a garrison of ten -- one officer and nine men and I was soon made senior in charge of others in spite of my youth. I was dedicated and spent much time in study of the rules and codes of practice of the army. I wanted to do well and get out of such a terrible place as Nazareth. My companions and fellow soldiers took rather a different view and inclined toward single-minded drinking and neglect of themselves. I wanted to do well. And be promoted. Even our officer -- Lucian -- had given up hope. For most of the others, Nazareth was the end of the road, the end of a career, the end. There was a saying, old even then "*Can anything good come out of Nazareth?*" For me it was, I hoped, just a beginning. It proved to be so.

The loneliness of such a camp life for a young man is hard to imagine for one who has not known it; to be miles from home, in the midst of a hard-to-understand people, who hate you and you hate them and to have only the companionship of your fellow soldiers. After six months I was ready to die. I would have done anything to get out of the miserable town. The longer one stays in such places the more attractive the local women become -- it is a well-known fact. Soon all the best and most well-meaning regulations, laws, and religious strictures mean nothing. They say that one never forgets the first girl -- and I suppose it is true for women also -- that one ever loved. I was stricken with one of the local girls. She was shy, beautiful, lovely. She was afraid of me and my companions but there were smiles exchanged and coy turnings away. I was much too inexperienced in those days to realize that we should press our courtship forthwith, but they were taking risks. I dare not now think what would have happened had we been discovered. Soon my friend -- Xanto -- and I would arrange to be in the vicinity of the stream where Mary and her cousin came late in the evening. There followed for me one of the most happy periods of my life in Judea. At last I had someone to talk to, someone who could explain things to me, and could see how bitterly lonely and unhappy I was. I was not as tough a soldier as I'd thought, although I'd been brought up for the army life. My father never told me about the excruciating pain of loneliness and the boredom of being garrisoned in small provincial towns.

The story is an old one, one of the oldest. In time Mary stopped coming for water and one day Xanto and I were met by her brothers who were demanding to know who was responsible for making her with child. In the fashion of young men I denied any part in the matter and we as Roman soldiers backed the Jewish boys down. Naturally we could not accept any responsibility and risk being brought up on charges. It would have been the end of me. I was ashamed to have to deny the girl but the plain fact was I could not be sure. If she was seeing me, perhaps she was seeing others.

The matter was dealt with rather quickly and quietly I thought. They married her to old Joseph the carpenter. I even went to the wedding as I had become convinced in my mind I had no responsibility in these matters. Joseph seemed so willing to take on a bride I was not sure he wasn't involved all along.

For my part, I was glad things were settled. Although looking back, I feel some regret. I loved her as perhaps you can only love when you are so young and so innocent and know nothing of life's suffering, pain and the irrationality of the world. While all of this was going on, I got what I'd wanted: promoted and reassigned to be the supervisor of tax collectors in charge of the census that was ordered by Augustus. I was sent to a larger town, Bethlehem. My job was to supervise the work of the Jewish tax collectors to be sure their rates were uniform, fair, and that they did not take too much for themselves.

I went down there with very little thought of the close call I'd had. Had I been named as the father of the child, I would have probably been discharged from service and forced to marry the girl. That is not the plan my father had for me or the plan I had for myself. Looking back now, I could probably have made it. But that was behind me. When I was in Bethlehem I set about getting things in order. The business was for every Judean to be counted in the census and a tax, based on total wealth, set, which would be sent to Rome. Our process was to use a local official as a tax collector under Roman supervision. Part of the money went to local administration and local public improvements, and part went to King Herod; 50 percent was taken for support of Rome directly. No fairer or better means of collecting taxes has ever been devised than the one sent out by Caesar Augustus. Every person in the district had to go to the town in which he was born and there be counted, enrolled and pay the tax. It was a good system.

I was glad to be in a larger town and have better accommodations. I stayed in a well-kept inn of about forty rooms and commanded five men in the process of administration. We began the census with the local residents and each day dispatched the money to Jerusalem where it was received and forwarded on to Rome. Every day for weeks people came into town from the countryside and from all parts of Judea to be enrolled. In the spring there was a great rush of people to Bethlehem to be enrolled because the time for paying the head tax without penalty was running out. For weeks the town was crowded and I had to call upon reinforcements to keep order.

And then, one day, I saw Mary again. She came into town with Joseph and he came up to the desk where we did the enrollment. He did not recognize me even when I intervened to question the assessment process of the enrolling officer. But she knew it was me and who I was. Joseph, no doubt, was like most of the Judeans who thought all Romans looked alike and paid no attention to us at all for fear of us. It was best that we did not see each other. It makes everything easier. Certainly no group of people were more despised by both Romans and Jews than the Jews who cooperated with the Romans, the tax collectors, and other petty officials.

Mary was quite pregnant. Months had passed. She seemed tired but happy sitting on her absurd donkey named Zeno. I knew they would have trouble finding accommodations so I suggested to Joseph that he go to the inn where I stayed and tell the innkeeper I said to make a place for them. Little did I know what was to follow. The strange events of the next day and night have been talked about a lot, but no one that I know who was there knows the whole of the story. There is perhaps no whole of the story to be learned.

The sight of the lovely Mary depressed me. My mind played over the loss of her, of what I'd had and what might have been. I was angry, resentful and terribly confused. I went to the inn and with a group of friends proceeded to get roaring drunk. I fought, shouted and sang all through the night. I was in a frenzy. Then in the early morning hours there began the strange music which seemed to come from nowhere. Everywhere there was singing.

Staying at the inn there were a mob of people, and they were all out back looking in the cave where the horses, cattle and sheep were stabled. There were shepherds, traders, all kinds of people and everyone seemed to be going out to the stable. There was a lot of talking about the Messiah, "*the promised one has come*", one of the shepherds told me. My first thought in all this was that it should be reported to Herod. He and others were concerned about any disturbing event. I feared a revolt. A revolt can be set off by any loose talk. When I heard them calling the event the birth of a new King of the Jews it practically sobered me up. I had to get up to go see what was going on and to see for myself. I went out to the stable and there I saw Mary, Joseph and the child.

"*What is it?*" I asked.

"It's a boy," I was told "and does surely look like his father." Everyone was agreed with that judgment and I satisfied myself of that.

"What was that strange music?"

It was shepherds singing they told me.

"But it was so strange and beautiful," I said.

The baby was very handsome and must have weighed seven pounds or more. There were all kinds of people in the place, far too many people. All crowding around - weeping, moaning, talking, carrying on.

About that time there came three men, emissaries or potentates from the East. A strange crew indeed dressed in fine clothes but dirty, even filthy. They came in with gifts for the baby and told the parents that they had been following a star for days and it had led them to the stable. I could not understand their language and I don't believe that Joseph and Mary could either, but anyone could understand the very beautiful gifts they had. I thought, "Old Joseph is lucky on this because he will not have to declare these items. They would fetch a pretty sum." I thought that this will be my contribution and let Rome be hanged on its share. The innkeeper and his son were upset by the crowds trooping through the inn and in his yards. They were trampling on his garden too. Some had been upbraiding him for putting the mother and child in a stable. He put them all out and put his young son as a guard at the door. It was about then that I realized that the family was in my horse's regular stable. My horse was outside in the cold. Of course, I'd sent word for the innkeeper to make a place for them. He was crowded and people were everywhere in the inn. I decided to go back inside and drink a toast of welcome to the little guy. And so I did. We had a grand celebration. I was forgetting Mary, the singing, the three Kings and the Messiah nonsense.

If I had a single fault, it is the fault of many soldiers who drink hard spirituous liquors -- I become maudlin and mean alternately, mixing self-pity with anger. And that anger may land upon anyone. That is why I've put it aside.

Before long it was morning; I'd been up all night and it was time to get up. I went out to get my horse and found the innkeeper's son standing guard and he launched into a story too smooth by half about my horse having just been brought outside. I grabbed him up playfully pretending to be angry and threatened to cut his tongue out. All at once I felt my arms pinned against my side by someone very strong. I was lightly released and the innkeeper and Joseph were there. It was Joseph who told me, indicating he did indeed know me *"Quintus, leave the boy alone. He is innocent. He is guilty of only kindness and acting on your instructions."*

The innkeeper offered to make it up to me by saying I would not have to pay. Nor my men either.

I felt foolish. Here I was acting a fool and because I was armed with the power of the Roman state they were speaking soft words to me to turn me away. It is no wonder that they did hate us so.

Yes, that is the part that I know about the birth of Jesus, the son of Mary and Joseph of Nazareth. And of all the stories that have been made up, don't take any of them as true. Lately we have heard much about that little boy who was born that night. Just five years ago he was executed for rebellion. Everywhere there are little groups of followers who claim him as the Messiah and Son of God sent for deliverance. My wife, Julia, who is Jewish, is greatly taken up with the idea. I have had three tours of duty in Judea, but the first is the one I remember. Especially the night of the exquisite singing, my loneliness and strange happiness when the baby was born in the stable. I never reported the incident of the foreign emissaries. Perhaps I should have.

Quintus

# AN OLD SHEPHERD REMEMBERS

We had come to Bethlehem like all the rest. A long hot dusty trip. People were crowded into the town. My father, my four brothers, and I had come with 1,600 sheep. We camped in the hills above the town along with the many others forced to come to be counted, enrolled, and taxed. My father was very angry about this, but he kept this anger to himself and in the family. He despised the Romans with their armies and their taxes. I cannot blame him, but I know both sides now; I have been a tax man and I now know how confused matters were forty, forty-five years ago, when Cyrenius was Governor and ordered everyone to be enrolled and taxed. We still work from the records made at that time. As a farmer with much land and a great deal of livestock, Father hated the tax.

I was only 11 or 12 -- my brothers Matthias, Simeon, Philemon and Saul -- were all older than me by seven years or more. They brought me along at the last minute. It was unusual that I should be taken on the sixty-two mile trip because I am lame -- from birth; it doesn't bother me, I just have to make an extra effort. People feel sorry for me, pity me, but it doesn't hurt. It's probably why I became a bookkeeper and a tax collector because I was considered unfit to do the work of a farmer by most people, especially my brothers.

My father never felt that way. He made me do everything that any other boy does. He did not want to see me "*soft*", and he feared if I did not learn to take care of myself that I should be "*eaten by the world.*" Still I knew that he felt sorry for me. Sometimes he would be drinking, visiting with friends and he would fall to telling stories about my mother and how I was born. I have heard him cry, shout and rage about it. The first time I heard it, I thought he was angry at me for being lame and killing my mother. But over time I heard the story many times and came to understand that he blamed himself. It was not until I was a man and a father of children that I understood. It frightened me as a child to hear his anger at me, at the Rabbis, at the governors, his friends, the Romans and at himself.

It was not often that he drank and gave vent to his anger. My father's name -- Simon. And I am called Noah bar Simon -- Noah, son of Simon. I was named for the just man who was the second father of the world.

It took us six days to bring the sheep the sixty miles. I don't now know why we were there with the sheep. I assume they were to be counted too.

Perhaps they were being sold as part of the trip. I just don't remember.

Bethlehem was like a carnival and a festival. People were everywhere, sleeping in the streets. Food was sold on the street corners - sweetmeats, roast lamb, bread. There were jugglers and shows. Men spoke to crowds of people selling them cloth and jewelry. I'd never seen so many people, so many kinds of people. Men argued and debated into the night. The whole place was bristling with ideas. For a young boy it was tremendously exciting and I got to see it all walking through the town with my father. He seemed to know everybody; everyone greeted him. It was a happy time. It seemed like a grand thing to do. I even dared to think that the Romans had a good idea in bringing people together.

At night in the hills we set our fires to keep the wolves away and to keep the chill of the night at bay. Some of the shepherds sang songs. The nights were bright and clear. It was so dry that if you rubbed the back of the sheep you'd make sparks fly.

The night that it happened -- the night of the star -- is a night I'll never forget. People still talk about it, people who weren't even there. That day -- I think it was the third or fourth day we'd been at Bethlehem -- we had a supper of lamb and my father brought an unusual bread from the town. After supper I went to my place to watch the sheep and I fell asleep just after dark. I was wrapped in my cloak. I dreamed as I slept that I could hear singing and that the night had become as bright as day, lighted by a star. I was awakened hours later hearing the fierce bleating of sheep under attack. I leaped up heading in the direction of the noise. I saw six or seven lambs scattered, bloody, dead and dying. All the sheep were raising a noise. I feared I should be punished for this. The task of a shepherd is to protect the sheep. My thoughts stopped. I came face to face with a huge wolf, head lowered for attack, snarling, growling and hot red eyes. It had not run away. No sound would come from my throat. I was so afraid at that moment that I lunged at the wolf with my staff but he stood his ground, rushed at me and I tumbled backward which let the sound out of my body -- "*Wolf!*" The wolf seized a middle-sized lamb. I rose to my feet and ran at the wolf beating and cursing it. The wolf ran away as my brothers Matthias and Saul came running up. Together we gathered the dead lambs, trying to save what we could. The noise of 1,600 fear-stricken and bleating sheep is an awesome sound. We passed back and forth through the flock calming them.

Six lambs were dead.  I wondered at the strength of the wolf, the wantonness of the killing. Wolves do not always kill this way.

We were trying to calm the sheep, but who was to calm me?  I told the story of what happened to my two brothers, then I told it again.  I told it to Simeon and Philemon.  Then I told it to my father.  The red-eyed snarling wolf biting into the lamb is a picture still with me.  My father said it could have happened to anybody.  "*Wolves will be wolves.  Don't fear wolves.  But fear the wolves among men.*"  By this I knew he meant the Romans, who as a race were suckled by a wolf.

Then it happened.  The night lit up.  The night which was windy and dry became cool and brightly lit by the star.  Our sheep grew quiet and even placid again.  You could hear singing, the singing of the shepherds, but then mixed with it and getting louder, was other singing.  It was beautiful.  And it was calming.

A shepherd from further up the hill came running down into our camp scrambling over the stones.

"*Did you get the wolf?  Did you see the wolf?*" he asked.

"*Yes. Noah saw the wolf and ran him off,*" my father told him.

The young man did not look like a shepherd.

"*I have not come just about the wolf but to tell you to follow the star. Go see the child that is born. One who is to be savior of our people.*"

My father said, "*What's going on? Is there trouble? Is there fighting?*"

"*No. Follow the star and see the child who is to be the Messiah. The Messiah is born.*"

The young man ran off to tell others. The singing grew louder and louder.

"*We should go see what is going on,*" Matthias my oldest brother, said. At about that time, six or eight other shepherds came up and asked us to go with them to the town.

My father and I stayed behind to tend the sheep. Before they were gone he said, "*You go on with them. You've had a hard night already.*"

I joined in the group which got larger and larger as we went along. The town was thronged with people. It was just like midday. No one was asleep. People were everywhere, laughing, yelling. There were fights. They had not heard the music it seems.

We came to an inn and someone up front demanded to see the Messiah. We were told "*It's out back.*" We went to the rear of the inn to the stable and there was a mob of people, passing in and out to get a look at the baby. I scrunched down to move through the crowd. I saw the mother and the child. But in the middle of the crowd were three kings or princes -- one a huge black man. He must have been seven feet tall. He wore a turban and in the center a diamond or maybe a ruby. They had gifts of jewels. I could not understand their language.

Then one of the shepherds told the little family that an angel had told us that this baby was the Messiah, the anointed one. As I remember it, they didn't say anything. The shepherd said the angel told them. He kept saying it over and over again.

I do remember that a boy no older than myself -- the innkeeper's son I believe -- told us all to get out. He made everyone get out of the stable and into the yard. You could hear the music, the singing and I wondered if I was the only one hearing it, because no one else was paying attention. The people were talking about taxes, and crops, the Romans, and they were arguing and making jokes. If the Messiah had come, would it be this way?

Then I was hungry and I went into the streets in search of that good bread to wrap around the roast lamb.

That was years ago. Everything is different now.

# THE MIDWIFE'S TALE

Her name was Zelomi. I'd heard of her for years. She was present at the birth of Yeshua in Bethlehem although she was from Nazareth. She was the Nazareth midwife to Mary the mother of our precious Yeshua. There were many stories about her. She had quite a reputation for being a difficult person and uncooperative. It was said she had a kindly spirit where women were concerned but held men in lesser esteem if not contempt. If indeed she was the midwife present at the birth it was important for us to get her story. Others had attempted to talk to her in the years since the execution of Yeshua but she did not comply. She was not a member of The Way, our way ... those who follow the Messiah and acknowledge he has come.

I was surprised she was still alive. She must be beyond her seventieth year of age. But stories persisted about this Zelomi. Anyone who went to Nazareth had some new tale from her. In the twenty years since the death of Yeshua there'd been so many stories and tales that Luke and James, the brother of Yeshua, were among those who wanted us to establish a true record. Of the original disciples none had known him from birth. Some even doubted he'd been "born" at all. In the earliest days of his death they expected him to come back to set all things right for the "end time." Now we know this was a misunderstanding of his true intent and purpose.

You no doubt have heard the story about the birth - the day the world stood still. Everyone knows of the Star and the Visitation of the Persian kings. Everyone knows of the great angelic hosts that sang along with the shepherds. There is the story about how the animals spoke at the birth. There are many stories but are they true? Those who hate us laugh and scoff at our stories for many tales make us look foolish.

I was excited because I was going down to Nazareth to see this Zelomi. She'd agreed to see me and to talk with me. I decided to take Josephus with me to write it down. I'd feel better if she was a follower, but we can learn much from those who do not believe but have knowledge. Tomorrow we go out to see her. Nazareth is a dusty, ugly, inhospitable little town. We tried to locate the home and workshop of Joseph and Yeshua. It is well known but people have ignored and rejected the name of Yeshua. They even spit at the name. "He brought nothing but trouble to us", one said to me. "*And now he has brought you.*" There are not many alive who could have known Yeshua but they pretend to know everything and nothing. The family of Joseph is large but they have little interest in Yeshua. It is, to me, very sad but it fulfills the prophecy of Isaiah that a "*prophet is without honor in his own town*".

We went to see Zelomi in the house of her son. It is very nice and comfortable. We were served food and drink. This is the story we were told. It is written as she spoke it. We read it back to her at the end to be sure she agreed.

"Yes. I was with Mary for the birth of her son Yeshua. My name is Zelomi. I am a midwife. I have been present at the birth of most of the people of Nazareth. My eldest daughter took up the work when I got too old. After she died my son's wife Miriam did the work. It is good work. My mother before me had the touch too. I no longer do the work although last week I had to go out in the night and I'd not lost the skill. It is always satisfying to get the baby, clean it off, and hand it back to the mother. Many things can go wrong, and they have for me, when a child cannot get its breath, or it lies too still in the womb or gets tangled in the cord. Nothing is assured in this world but we are always sad when the labor results in a stillbirth. Women have much to suffer in this world, but it is the way the world goes on."

(I interrupted her here to ask if she would tell us about the birth of Yeshua in Bethlehem in the time of the census.)

"It was like any other birth except we'd gone to Bethlehem for the enrollment. It was called a census but it was really just a way to tax us Jews. You went to the census table - women and men - and gave your name and age and a <u>coin</u>, a gold coin that went straight into Herod's treasury. What a devil that man was! They counted the coins and that way they knew how many people there were. God forbade Jews to be counted but the Roman's did anything they pleased. They had no respect for us. They lived among us in those days, with a hatred and contempt for our life and ways that exceeds anything you could imagine. You are too young. In those days the gold coin was hard to come by. People today travel and throw money around. I don't know how they live. Money was scarce and life was hard in those days."

(I interrupted again, to get her on the story of Yeshua.)

"Yes. Yes. I know. You followers of The Way have been here before. You seem nice but some are so ignorant and twisting of words. They say I am a conjurer, sorcerer, spell giver. The ignorant always blacken the name of those they don't understand.

"It started with Joseph. I knew him, his first wife, a wonderful woman, and delivered their children. I was always surprised when after the wife died that he was selected by Mary's family to be the "father" of the baby. Yes, there was a great controversy about who the father was when she became pregnant. I can only tell you what I know. This town was full of gossip, tales and lies then and now. After Mary's father was unable to wrench the name of the boy with whom she'd lain, the mother decided on poor Joseph, the widower. I say 'poor Joseph' because he never knew what was going on, until he was married. The mother was skillful in managing men, she knew how to promise, imply, cajole and flatter them. Joseph did not seem all that reluctant even after he knew she was pregnant. He was a strong Jew, I can say that for him, and he never believed all of the crazy stories that Elizabeth, Anne and the other kinswomen of the little Mary made up. I came into it as the midwife. I think she believed the story, but she also came to love Joseph and respect him. She realized he'd been tricked. I always thought the man who'd been with her and was the father was the Roman soldier, Quintus, who was quartered in their home. He was a handsome man. He could not be named as the father because he'd have been punished by the Roman authorities. It was absolutely forbidden for soldiers to take up with the local women. And for our part, no decent women would sleep with a Roman soldier. But young people will do many unapproved things.

"It never mattered to me who was the father. I always say the child - boy or girl - looks like the father. And it does, even if the husband is not the father. It makes for peace and I get my fee more easily. Even in cases where there are severe doubts, reasons to question the father, one should welcome the child. *"Oh, it looks like its father"*. It flatters the man and eases his mind and any doubts that may have been present. It is best. For all practical purposes he will have to raise the children, so why confuse things. Who knows the truth of anything? This world would shatter and break if we knew all the secrets of people.

"So I came into it as the midwife. If ever a young girl needed a woman from outside her family, it was Mary. Her family were religious fanatics and given to seeing visions and hearing voices. But a baby is not a dream or an idea but a human child that needs nurture to get born and care afterwards. I tried to teach her the ways of women and mothers so she could care for her baby. Her own kin were no help.

"When the census order came to go up to Bethlehem, Joseph and Mary asked me to go because her time was close. Joseph's older sons, Simon and James, and their wives and children, went with us in the same party. It was my first time to be away from Nazareth and Joseph paid me very well to make the trip. It was somewhat difficult for Mary. She rode in the donkey cart with its constant jostling. That brought on the birth.

"Bethlehem was a mad house. It was called and still is called "The City of David". Every Jew wants to be related to David - as if it made any difference. But for this census the town was crowded. The arrangement for lodging Joseph had made was not honored. We were late in the night arriving and the innkeeper, having no way of knowing we would actually arrive, had let the room to others. It was a dark time. We arrived tired. I thought we'd have to sleep in the streets where the noise, drinking and gambling was uncontrollable. Even the Roman soldiers had given up keeping order. The innkeeper suggested the stable, as a place out of the wind and weather for the nine of us and the animal - we gladly took it. No sooner had we got settled than the baby came with a rush. All the jostling and excitement brought on the labor. The child was a boy and quite beautiful. He had the caul covering him. I washed him, tied off the cord and handed him to Mary who awakened to take him but then soon fell asleep again.

"Who did the child look like? You may ask. He looked like his father and mother. Men are so vain to expect a child looks like them when it is the mother who does the work.

"I was glad Mary and the baby slept for it gave us all a chance to get food from the inn. And little did we know of what was to come.

"The birth was easy. The child came quickly. And it was unusual in one way. I'd always had a stiff hand, the left hand that pained me in cold weather. The pain was in the joints and sometimes kept me from sleep. Not since that night have I had any pain. Yes, the baby cleaned up nice. He was all there - ten fingers, ten toes, and hearty cry. That's what you want. A child undeformed, uncrippled, like others, so he can make his way in the world.

"Joseph named him Yeshua. He was a good, quiet child. It was normal in every way except for the caul*.

"When people heard a baby had been born, they started coming. They must have thought we'd done it for their amusement. The innkeeper's little boy spread the word. Then other guests told of it. People brought gifts and gold coins. Everyone was congratulating Joseph. All the sons of David were impressed that gathered for the big family reunion. There was a new son of David born. Men began loud talking and the drinking of toasts. They were stomping around in everything. I had to run them out of the stable and into the night. Men are such fools. They were all pressing stories on Joseph and drinks, telling where they came from and their children. They were trying to fix their ties to one another - who knew who. They were all cousins. And gambling on everything. The animals did not seem to be a part of the festivities so they got put out in the open air. They put up a howl. Another family of travelers had to be taken in.

"The night was bright. The wine flowed. Gifts were given. Through it all the child and the mother slept.

"Oh yes, they talked of the child as a new king of Israel, like David. And the shining stars were named as evidence of great things. People from all over came in with gifts of oil and sweet herbs. I rubbed the child down.

"That's the way it happened. I've heard some of the stories but I can tell you it was like this. It was an easy birth and sweet in the way that Joseph , Mary and the whole family welcomed the child. The celebrating sons of David with their gifts were not welcomed by me. Their noise and drinking, carousing, laughter and coarse jokes disgusted me. Joseph had to pay the census coin for the child the next day.

The next night those foreigners, Persians, did come to see the child. They were in town and heard of this special child. They, as you know, place great reliance on the stars and read messages in them. We couldn't understand their language but they were very curious. The beautiful carved wood boxes they gave as gifts were lost or stolen before we got back home.

"There's more. I saw the child grow up. He was a bright and lively lad and Mary's family made a pet of him. He was spoiled by his grandmother but he was very able, even wise and did not let her influence go to his head. He was a happy lad and a very good carpenter from the earliest days of his apprenticeship. He traveled to many towns to do work even before he took up his "end of the world talk". Yes, we knew all about that. He'd said it many times. He felt the world was coming to an end, that God was going to sweep away the evil of men. We'd heard it all. We'd heard it before. What always surprised me is that others listened to it. He could make people believe things. But we'd heard from him and his family for years.

"I knew his mother all her life. I delivered her other children - six in all. She was sick, unto death when he got into trouble in Jerusalem. Its a wonder his whole gang wasn't killed. The Romans don't like people trying to take over where they rule.

(I asked her if she ever heard him preach.)

"Yes, I heard him when he came here to see his mother just before he got into all the trouble. I know his father was upset with him. He spoke here in the synagogue and in the field outside of town. I thought he was right about the poor in  spirit and the meek and the righteous and about love. But those are just fine words.

"Men just go on killing without any thought that they are killing some mother's child. I never look at a person that I have helped birth and not know there are miracles that come out of pain and suffering.

"That's all I have to say. I'm tired."

We read it back to her.

We left confused about the story but satisfied that Yeshua's birth in Bethlehem was an event that shook the world. It confirmed much we already knew.

* The caul is a part of the amniotic sac that sometimes covers the child's head. It is taken to be a sign of great good fortune and spiritual power. It's rare, occurring once in 10,000 births.

# THE FIRST CHRISTMAS AFTER THE WAR

The war was over in 1945, and we moved into our new home over the dry goods store my father brought after 22 years of selling shoes *"for the other man."* I was ten that year and I wanted a bicycle, but there weren't any. It wasn't as if we were poor, but there just weren't any available. Steel production and manufacturing had been carefully explained to me. There were just not any available. Steel had won the war. Steel was needed for other things. I read in the paper that Sears got fifty bicycles and they were sold out in five minutes. A lot of boys and girls wanted bikes that first Christmas after the war. I put the thought out of mind and knew that it would be another year before I could get a bike that would let me get the paper route I wanted. A year seems like such a long time.

Two days before Christmas, Daddy told me I should go with him the next day -- Sunday and Christmas Eve - to help deliver some bags of groceries to the widows of the Masons of the Dolcito Lodge #527 F & AM of the Grand Lodge of Alabama.

Sunday after church we took up our errand of calling on the widows. We saw an assortment of older women, some of whom needed the help and who got a cash gift too, and some who were only being remembered.  One of the ladies commented on "*what a smart young man*" I was, as I brought in the boxes of groceries.  It was pleasant work and it gave me a feeling of being helpful and of making Christmas a little brighter for these poor old ladies.

The day drew to a close but we still had another widow to call on.  It was just after 5 o'clock as we headed down the road to the last stop.  It was dark.  It was getting colder and colder.

This was our last stop of the day.  The lady was not a widow of a Mason.  My father called her a grass-widow and explained that her husband "*had run off*," and she was left with five children.  "*She needs the help*," he said so gruffly, I thought he might be angry with me.  We had in the car a box full of clothes and shoes, dungarees, flannel shirts, socks, dresses for children of all ages, two bags of groceries, a box of canned goods, and apples, oranges, and pecans.

We drove nearly 30 miles to a place far back in the county.  We left the black top at Pinson and we're on dirt roads for the last few miles.  We stopped in the middle of a field.  It was dark as we cut out across the field to the house where a light dimly glimmered in the window.  We were loaded down with groceries - I was carrying the turkey and Daddy had the canned goods.

Daddy had met the man who had run off when he came into our store to buy school clothes in September. He'd just gotten on at the pipe shops and was hoping to charge the clothes. He was a veteran and had been dressed in the khaki of the mustering out. Daddy had wanted to help a veteran so he let him have the school clothes, some work pants and chambray shirts, and a pair of brogans, work shoes for the man. We didn't charge things at the store - we were cash and carry and believed that was the way to do business - no books to keep and no bills to send, but for a vet - well "*you have to give a little for the boys who have been over there.*"

I remembered the man -- he talked loud and bragging. I thought of him as we trudged along toward the house where he'd lived and no longer lived. He'd been a thin, sallow-faced man; he looked tired and he talked with the harsh accents of a country man. He was giving up working his land and farming and was going to work at the pipe shop. He bought clothes for all of the children and told us that his wife was pregnant. I remembered that -- she was going to have a baby. I took all this in as I swept the floor, which was my job.

A dog barked as we neared the house. It was a big dog, a black and white spotted dog that looked mean. Daddy picked up a rock and scared him off.

We knocked on the door and the woman came to the door carrying a baby and a coal oil lamp. She was taken aback a bit, and so was I, for the baby was nursing at the mother's breast. I'd often seen black women doing this out in front of the A&P on Saturdays when everybody came to town.

"*Mrs. Gilliam?*" my father asked. "*I'm here from the Masons and have some Christmas for you and the children. We heard you were on hard times. . .*" His voice kind of trailed off as behind the woman we saw grouped a whole assortment of dirty-faced boys and stringy-haired girls who seemed to be miniatures of the woman. They were wearing only underpants, except one girl who had on a flour sack dress of a pattern I knew from having worked around my uncle's feed store all summer. It was a Jim Dandy hog feed sack.

The woman at first had said nothing but began in a slow and halting way to mutter apologies. The floor behind was all dirt and I could see the newspapers that were used as wallpaper. I knew these were poor people. The smell of the house was strong -- that mixture of cooking fat, dirt, and human odor that knocks you over.  You can smell it in the city tenements and projects now and wherever there is poverty.

We went in and set out things down on the floor and bed.  There was no table.  A small fire burned in the stove in the center of the floor.

"*Run back out to the car and get the rest of the stuff,*" Daddy told me.  "*We've got some clothes and shoes for the kids.*"

"*Let Sealy go with him,*" Mrs. Gilliam said.  The little girl in the flour sack dress went with me.  She was barefooted.  The two of us went out to the car and got the other bags and boxes of clothes and a couple of toys that someone had given us.  We didn't say anything to each other.  I didn't know what to say.

We were thanked and thanked and the woman began to cry.  Daddy and I left the things and then kind of hurried back to the car.  We drove back down the way we'd come and I looked out at the cold night and began wondering what I'd get for Christmas.

I asked Daddy why the man had run off.  "*Too much for him, son.  Some men just can't face their responsibilities.  He's just plain sorry.*"

"*What'll they do when the food's all gone?*" I asked.

It was quiet for a while and I never got an answer to that question.

Christmas came as it always does no matter how long it takes when you are ten. I remember that we had Hershey bars that year -- the first Christmas after the war.

I got up early but waited before tearing into the packages for I knew I had to wait till everybody was up. My brother was the baby and he was the one we waited to see "*what Santa Claus had brought.*" Opening the packages, I got books and clothes (we owned a clothing store). A boy who's ten doesn't need toys anymore.

It was nice, but the bicycle I'd hoped for wasn't there. It had been explained to me that there was a shortage of steel and they just didn't have bicycles for sale in the stores. I'd expected a miracle but I was glad to have a Monopoly set.

Daddy was putting some coal in the Warm Morning heater and said to me, "*Take this scuttle and go out and get some coal, boy.*" He startled me a little bit because it was my job to keep plenty of coal in the house and I kept extra scuttles in our big hall. I jumped to it and opening the door to the big hall, I ran into the shiniest red bicycle I'd ever seen -- a Roadmaster.

It was the greatest surprise of my life and lives in the annals of my family which cannot pass a Christmas without recalling the time I was ten. It is told and retold how I looked, how I gasped, and how I was beside myself in a way untypical for me then -- and now. Speechless.

That Christmas day I rode my bike all over town and beyond town into the country. It is a freeing experience to have a bike and to be able to go as you please. Sometimes when I rode my bicycle over the town and along the dirt roads around the town, I'd think about the woman with the children -- and the girl who was just my age -- and I'd think about the man who'd run off and wonder what did they do when the food was gone.